Library Guild

RIGHT ALONG!

A COWBOY NAMED ERNESTINE

BY NICOLE RUBEL

Dial Books for Young Readers

New York

Published by Dial Books for Young Readers
A division of Penguin Putnam Inc.
345 Hudson Street
New York, New York 10014

Designed by Nancy R. Leo-Kelly
Text set in Minister
Printed in Hong Kong on acid-free paper
1 3 5 7 9 10 8 6 4 2

Library of Congress Cataloging-in-Publication Data
available upon request

The artwork for this book was created with black ink and colored markers.

———————————————

*Many little animals are shown throughout this book, including
an armadillo on every page. See how many you can find.*

"You are never a quitter until you quit trying."

Dora Rhoads Waldrop (Born 1911)

ERNESTINE O'REILLY, with hair as wild and red as campfire flames, came all the way from County Clare, Ireland, to Lizard Lick, Texas, as a mail-order bride. She stepped down from the stagecoach, straightened her best hat, and looked for her husband-to-be.

A figure like a tumbleweed on stilts shambled up. There wasn't a single hair on his head, but below his nose was nothing *but* hair, making a mighty effort to reach his knees. A squirt of tobacco juice landed at Ernestine's feet.

He said, "Come on, girl," and grabbed her hand.

Ernestine snatched it back, saying, "Begging your pardon, but it's Virgil Beetle I'm waiting for."

"That's me. Enough courtin', now, we got to get back."

Ernestine hadn't come this far to let a little thing like a bad first impression stop her, so she was soon bumping along in a buckboard to the Broken Spoke Ranch. When they arrived, Virgil's three brothers, Wilbur, Crusty, and Ned, came out to meet them. So did Ned's wife, Prunella.

"Where's the preacher?" Virgil asked.

"He went to Gopher Gulch for a hangin'. Won't be back for a week," Ned explained.

"Shoot, I done went and washed up for the wedding," Virgil grumbled.

"Well, I didn't count on getting married today anyway," Ernestine said. "How about some dinner?"

"You'll be fixin' it," said Prunella. "And after dinner you'll be sleepin' in the barn."

Ernestine went inside the house. There wasn't a clean dish or surface in the place. "Makes the barn sound downright homey," she said.

At dinner the Beetles started gobbling food before Ernestine even set the table, not a one waiting for a fork or spoon. When Ernestine finally sat down, there was nothing left except some gnawed chicken wings, and the bluetick hound snatched those.

"I've seen neater pigs and more courteous donkeys than this family," she said as she cleaned up again.

Soon Ernestine was sorry she had ever heard of the Beetle family. Every day the boys got dirtier and Prunella got meaner. "What will I do?" Ernestine fretted. "I don't have enough money to return to Ireland, but there must be a way home."

When the preacher came, Ernestine claimed she had to get her mother's lucky garter. "A girl just can't get married without something old, something clean, something borrowed, something green," she said, and she went inside the house. She quickly changed into Virgil's clothes, ones that she had just washed, of course. It took five pairs of socks to make his boots fit. She twisted her hair into a knot and covered her head with his Sunday Stetson. Then she snuck out the back door.

Baby Virgil

After two days in the hot Texas sun, she was so thirsty that the cactus were beginning to look friendly. In a daze she headed for a bit of shade and walked smack into the side of a longhorn.

When she came to, a cowboy was holding a canteen to her lips. He flashed a grin brighter than a shooting star and whiter than the moon.

"What's your name, son?" he asked.

"Er-Ernesti—" she stammered.

"You don't sound like a Texan, Ernest T."

"It's from Ireland I've come."

"Well, I'm from west of the Pecos, and on account of my pearly-whites they call me Texas Teeth," he said with a grin that a beaver would envy. "You look scrawny as a coyote pup. Come on over to the chuck wagon and help yourself."

Baby-face Bill, the cook, fed Ernestine beans and biscuits washed down with cold coffee. She thought it was heavenly. "Eats kind of dainty-like, don't he?" said Bill.

Ernestine spit and wiped her mouth on her sleeve to look tougher.

FLOUR
GOLD CROWN

FLOUR
GOLD CROWN

"Can you herd cattle, Ernest T.? We're a man short and could use some help,"
said Texas Teeth.
"I've herded sheep on my father's farm," she said.
"Close enough for me," said Texas Teeth.

Texas Teeth taught her how to throw a lasso, and soon Ernestine could hog-tie a calf with the best of them. Riding was a bit harder, but after a few days she didn't fall off more than twice an hour. She kept her hat on and pretended to shave every morning.

At first the other hands seemed a rowdy bunch. The Pirate wore an eye patch. Cactus Pete was fond of the juice of prickly pears. A small man with beady dark eyes was known as Greasy Weasel.

But at night around the campfire, even the most ornery buckaroo loved to listen to cowboy stories. They took turns telling the wildest tall tales they could imagine. Greasy Weasel told some of the best. Not to be outdone, Ernestine spun a tale called "Turtle Soup."

"Once, a lad, pardon, a cowboy named Freckles decided to round up all the turtles in Texas and sell them in El Paso for a fortune.

"When his herd was big as a box canyon, he hit the trail. The turtles had to keep stopping because of their tender feet, so he shod them with special iron shoes.

"The herd moved steady until they came to a creek. Iron shoes are too heavy for swimming, and the turtles drowned. So Freckles dammed the creek, threw in heated rocks until the water boiled, and had enough turtle soup to feed all of Texas. He never made his fortune, but he had a fine meal."

"Turtle Soup" became the most popular story of the drive, popular with everyone except Greasy Weasel.

Finally, in a whirlwind of dust and bawling calves, they brought the herd into Abilene. Texas Teeth gave the hands their wages. Ernestine's share still wasn't enough to get her back to Ireland.

"Come on, Ernest T.!" said Texas Teeth, slapping her on the back. "Let's go have a little fun." Ernestine didn't feel much like celebrating, but she went along to town. That's where she heard about the Third Annual Abilene Roping and Riding Rodeo Competition.

"I bet I can out-rope and out-ride any buckaroo here," said Texas Teeth. "You can hog-tie a calf pretty as a Christmas present, Ernest T. Why don't you give it a try? Could earn some good cash."

"Sure," she said. "Even if I lost, I'd be no worse off than before." So when Texas Teeth signed up for calf roping, she added her name, "Ernest T. O'Reilly," to the list. But Greasy Weasel was watching, his face as sour as spoiled milk. "That redheaded boy's getting too big for his britches," he said. And when no one was looking, he switched Ernestine's name from calf roping to bull riding.

Ernestine jumped off the fence when her number was called, and followed a cowboy to a stall. As she looked down at a wicked set of horns, she knew something was terribly wrong. "Wait, I'm to do calf roping, not bull riding!" she cried. "'Tis a terrible mistake you're making!"

The rodeo hands laughed. "That's what they all say, kid," she was told as they lowered her onto the bull.

The chute popped open, the bull burst out, and the crowd roared. The bull snorted and bounced like it had springs for legs. Ernestine clung on for a few seconds, but the bull kicked both hind legs at the sky, and she sailed over the fence. Ernestine went one way, her hat another, and her red hair spread out around her head like wildfire. Luckily, she landed in a big, soft pile of horse apples.

The audience gasped, "It's a girl!"

Texas Teeth rode over and said, "Didn't know you were a bull rider! I reckon there's a lot of things I don't know about you, Ernest T., or should it be Ernestine now?"

"That would be Miss O'Reilly to you, you cackling goose! If you weren't on that horse, I'd—"

"You'd what?" asked Texas Teeth.

"I'd do this!" she shouted, and pulled him off his horse smack into the middle of the manure pile. Texas Teeth sat laughing at her, until Ernestine had to laugh too. Then he gave her a kiss big as the Texas sky.

Abilene had a full-time preacher, so Ernestine and Texas Teeth were married that Sunday. Both bride and groom cleaned up right nice. Ernestine wore cowboy boots and a dress trimmed with Irish lace. Texas Teeth wore a new suit with buttons as pearly as his teeth. They settled down on a neat little ranch by the Pecos and soon had a fine crop of children with fiery red hair and sparkling white teeth. And their favorite bedtime story was "Turtle Soup."